To Steve, my favorite cook
— M.S.

To Rosie and "Sigh"
— M.P.

Dial Books for Young Readers
An imprint of Penguin Random House LLC, New York

Text copyright © 2020 by Marilyn Singer
Illustrations copyright © 2020 by Marjorie Priceman

Visit us at penguinrandomhouse.com

Printed in China • ISBN 9780735227903 • 10 9 8 7 6 5 4 3 2 1

Design by Jennifer Kelly • Text set in New Baskerville ITC

The illustrations in this book are done in gouache, linolcum block printing, and collage.

Thanks to Brenda Bowen, Lucia Monfried, and the whole Penguin crew for serving up this book. — M.S.

Follow the Recipe

Poems About Imagination, Celebration & Cake

by
Marilyn Singer

illustrated by
Marjorie Priceman

Dial Books for Young Readers

recipe for a good recipe

What's in a good recipe?

Something right for me and you.

Steps to follow, *A to Z.*

What's in a good recipe

for falling in love, for making a stew,

for balance or for harmony?

What's in a good recipe?

Something right for me and you.

Pot Luck Vegetable

1 c. onion, chopped
2 yel. squash
4 cloves garlic, minced
3 c. baby spinach

Place vegetables i...
Cook on H. for...
Add spinach at...

Secret Recipe

recipe for success in cooking

Crack your eggs when you're happy.

Beat them well when you're glad.

Melt your butter in a saucepan.

Take your eggs and gently add.

Stir them slowly till they're scrambled.

Serve them to your mom and dad.

Things taste best when you are cheerful.

Never cook when you are mad.

recipe for measurement

Smidgen, pinch, dash,

drop, jigger, gill.

How much to put in?

How much to fill?

Scant, rounded, heaping,

level, sifted, packed

(firmly or lightly).

Must you be exact?

Grams, drams, and ounces,

a soupçon, a cup.

You need to see a glossary

so you don't mess things up.

But once you make a recipe

more than once or twice,

trust your tongue to tell you

if you need to be precise.

recipe for patience

*Please, peas
be patient, please*

Take three pounds of peas

unzip a pod

remove each pea one by one

gently toss into a pot

plink

plink

plink

plink

Celeriac
Yum
I'm
R
I

Begin again

and again till the

plink

plink

plink

becomes the softer

pluh

pluh

pluh

the gentle thrill

as the pot begins to fill

plink plink

Splash!!

plink, plink

plink, plink

Splash!!!

A gnarly, nubbly vegetable.

You can't identify it.

Celeriac? Kohlrabi?

It doesn't matter. Try it!

A fruit that's oddly colored,

that's spiky, waxy, hairy.

A lychee or a rambutan.

There's no need to be wary.

Some say it's much more daring

to go skiing or canoeing.

But great adventures may begin

when you're boldly chewing.

yum

Delicious!! I am a Lychee

te like a grape! I am a Rambutan. My name means "hair".

Recipe for

recipe for
balance

Too much water

Too much flour

Too much sweet

Too much sour

Too much inside

Too much out

Too much whisper

Too much shout

Too much slowness

Too much rush

Too much rock-hard

Too much mush

Too much nerve

Too many fears

Too many jokes

Too many tears

Too much sleepy

Too awake

Much too salty

chocolate cake

Although sometimes,

you're bound to fail,

keep measuring—

and use a scale.

recipe for a poem

Choose your words carefully,

    selecting only the freshest ingredients.

Also your similes, your metaphors.

Don't scatter them haphazardly

    like grains of rice tossed at a wedding.

Trim all the fat.

But do include

    a hint of honey,

    a bit of bitter rind,

    a pinch of spice—

some delicious surprise.

Take care on the page,

    as you would on the plate:

We eat first with our eyes.

recipes for enjoying the seasons

Summer

Lemonade. If I

 had a butterfly's tongue, I'd

never need a straw.

Autumn

Pomegranate seeds:

 In fall, I am rich enough

to dine on rubies.

Winter

Icicles hanging

     from the pine tree. After school,

choose a free dessert.

Spring

Asparagus spears

     appear, grand marshals leading

the parade of green.

improvise

recipe for
following recipes

Sometimes you must follow things strictly word for word.

Sometimes it's more lively if you improvise.

The tried and true may sometimes be exactly what's preferred.

Sometimes you must do it strictly word for word.

Tuna fish and caramel would surely be absurd.

But sweet potato pizza? An excellent surprise!

Sometimes you must follow things strictly word for word.

Sometimes it's more lively if you improvise.

Experim

recipe for social studies

There's a tale worth telling in every dish,

waiting hungrily for us to share—

a potpourri of history to sample if we wish.

How the Chinese gave us noodles, the Japanese raw fish.

Why pizza and hot dogs are popular fare.

There's a tale worth telling in every dish.

Who brought us the tasty potato knish?

Why was eating tomatoes once considered a dare—

a potpourri of history to sample if we wish.

Nupoleon Bonaparte loved his licorice.

And King Henry VIII, his fine roasted pear.

There's a tale worth telling in every dish.

What made President John Adams vinegarish?

Is it true that Cleopatra put honey in her hair?

A potpourri of history to sample if we wish!

Just when do eggs turn devilish?

And what makes caviar so rare?

There's a tale worth telling in every dish—

a potpourri of history to sample if we wish.

recipe for Love

recipe for love

He's the apple of your eye.

He's a sugarplum.

She is such a peach,

makes you want to hum.

He's the cherry on top

of your favorite ice cream.

You go bananas

when you see her.

She's a honey, she's a dream.

School lunches now are no longer pallid.

Love makes the most delicious fruit salad!

recipe for disaster

It's the open bag of flour on the edge of a shelf.

It's the soy sauce, not vanilla, in the pumpkin pie.

The fancy cheese soufflé that you tried to make yourself.

The jalapeño pepper that you rubbed into your eye.

It's wrestling with your brother by the restaurant buffet.

It's a pitcher full of grape juice and someone's new white shirt.

The time you were a turkey in the Christmas play

and stumbled off the stage (though you didn't get hurt).

It's the sandwiches Dad makes with his mystery meat.

It's the twenty-dollar bill that you watched your beagle swallow.

It's dreaming of spaghetti—but you're munching on your sheet.

It's the nightmare recipe that you never want to follow!

recipe for science

This kitchen
is
your laboratory:
combining
molecules,
forming
crystals,
growing
good microbes.
Pickling
cucumbers.
Cool!
Assembling
rock candy.
Sweet!
Scrambling
eggs.
Fresh!
What's cooking?
Science!

Science,
what's cooking?
Fresh
eggs
scrambling.
Sweet
rock candy
assembling.
Cool
cucumbers
pickling.
Good microbes
growing.
Crystals
forming.
Molecules
combining.
Your laboratory
is
this kitchen!

recipe for endurance

Think of a time before blenders and mixers,
electrical fixers.

Think of a time before microwaves, stoves,
when there wasn't sliced bread, only freshly baked loaves.

Keep stirring the pot.

Picture the chance to strengthen a limb
without going to Gym.

Think of porridge or pudding or maybe risotto
back in the day and use this as your motto.

Lots of things change. Some do not.
Think of endurance—you still need it a lot.
And keep stirring the pot.

recipe for fairy tales

Take three bowls of porridge (too hot, too cold, just right)

a gingerbread house

an apple Snow White shouldn't eat

a basket of goodies for Grandma

a handful of magical beans

a gathering of ramps (whatever that means)

a single pea.

make a wish

Once upon a time in a

Put in several witches

princesses, giants

a boy with a lamp

an ugly duckling

a cat that can talk

a humongous bean stalk

a juniper tree.

They don't have to be fancy.

They don't have to rhyme.

But you'll implore,

you'll ask for more

"once upon a time."

READING

recipe for reading

A book can be an entrée.

A book can be dessert.

Rich as a stew, airy as a soufflé.

A book can be cheesy.

A book can be please-y.

Something to eat carefully

or devour in big bites

during the days

or deep dark nights.

Topped with whipped cream, or served over rice.

Try it with a dash of spice.

Try it plain, multi-grain, with sesame seeds.

Whichever you choose, a book always feeds.

recipe for originality

To be unique, there's no quick fix:

Make your cakes from scratch.

Do not use someone else's mix.

To be unique, there's no quick fix:

Invent your own delicious tricks.

Put yourself in every batch.

To be unique, there's no quick fix:

Make your cakes from scratch.

recipe for memories

Sometimes it's just a sharp whiff of mustard,
and you recall being at the ballpark.
The sight of a cone dripping custard,
and you're there at the fair after dark.

The sound of corn popping—movies with Dad.
The buzz of the mixer when Grandma bakes pies.
The soup that Mom serves the day you're feeling bad.
The birthday surprise of your grandpa's French fries.

The too much red pepper that caused you to sneeze.
The store where you thought you'd bite into a lime.
The slushy you drank till it made your brain freeze.
The stories that start, "And then there was that time . . ."

Today becomes last week, June, July, December.
Food has the power to help you remember.

CAPE HATTERAS, NORTH CAROLINA

recipe for magic

A dish
of strawberry
ice cream taken outside.
Fireflies spangle the air, coolly
twinkling.

A slice
of pumpkin pie
served by warming firelight.
Outside a barred owl is madly
hooting.

recipe for substitution

A newspaper won't keep you dry in the rain.

An air freshener isn't a lovely perfume.

A leaf's not so great if you must blow your nose.

Your dog's crate is fun, but not much of a room.

But . . . dental floss can cut a soft piece of cheese.

A paper bag helps ripen all kinds of fruit.

Try zucchini for pasta and lettuce for bread.

Learn what you can—and cannot—substitute!

recipe for courage

There's always a chance to be brave,

to choose a bold way to behave:

Tasting your very first bagel with lox.

Returning a bullied kid's mango juice box.

Delivering rice and beans to feed

hundreds of people badly in need

at home or in a foreign land.

To take a risk, to take a stand,

with something light or something grave,

there's always a chance to be brave.

recipe for understanding

Share bread,

share histories—

dense, chewy tales that take

time to rise. Crisp sketches as light

as air.

Share bread,

share histories—

loaves baked so long ago

or served up fresh from the oven

today.

Share bread:

bammy, brioche,

chapati or lavash . . .

Pass it around the table. Share

the world.

recipe for celebration

To celebrate your life each day,

laugh and enjoy your food.

That's what wise ones say.

It's a game we all can play:

Delight in everything you've chewed

to celebrate your life each day.

If there's no sunshine, be the ray.

Laugh—and you can change the mood.

That's what wise ones say.

Enjoy the worldwide grand buffet,

Broiled or boiled or barbecued,

to celebrate your life each day.

It may sound like some old cliché.

But it's the truth, you'll soon conclude.

That's what wise ones say.

You'll make the very best gourmet

When you've got zest and gratitude

to celebrate your life each day.

That's what wise ones say.